Love Monster & the Perfect Present

Rachel Bright

HarperCollins Children's Books

This monster...

(Hello, Love Monster.)

...thinks THIS monster...

is the most perfect monster in the world.

Yes, they are the bestest of friends.

(Aaaaah,
monsters.)

They spend each and every day together.
Sometimes doing fun stuff outside.

Sometimes
doing fun
stuff inside.

And Sometimes...

doing nothing
at all.

But there is one day in Cutesville, where these particular monsters live, that is different to all the others.

L CALENDAR
TOMORROW
decorate Cutesville with lights
TODAY
plan music for special day
RDAY
do nothing together
AGES AWAY
outside
AGES AWAY
plan rest of year
plan
DAY AFTER THE DAY AFTER SPECIAL DAY
play outside
THE FUTURE
Silver Clothes
(otherwise the same)
ONE DAY
go to moon
ONE DAY SOON
skipping
GES + WAY
Dentist

A VERY special day, in fact,
when the streets are filled with lights,
the air is filled with music...

and the whole town gets SUPER excited.

Yes, once a year in Cutesville it's...

PRESENT DAY

when everyone gives a lovely someone something lovely...

to show how special they are.

It's pretty much the best day ever.

So why does this monster look so worried?

Well, this year, Love Monster wanted to give a certain someone

something PERFECT...

...the most perfect present in the world.

But finding such a thing is not easy.

Hmmmmm... It was time to think very hard and to...

GO SHOPPING!
KER-CHING ENTERPRISES
PLANET PRESENT
OOOOH
PRESENT DAY
i-FAD!
SPECIAL OFFERS!
TOYS!
COME IN!
SPEND SPEND SPEND
CUTESEO DRIVE

And, oh! The shops were FULL OF HUNDREDS OF WONDERFUL, SHINYFUL things!

SPARKLY!
Y-BOX
Y-BOX
OOOOH! FREE BRILLIANT GAMES WITH EVERY BOX!
THE MOST FUN YOU CAN HAVE INSIDE!
COOL HAT!
COOL!
LOOK!
CUTE TEDDY!
DESIGNER STAR SHADES! You'll be so much cooler!
FUN GAME!
Y-Box Games
WORLD'S FASTEST TRAINERS

Love Monster was SURE he'd come to the right place!

But as it turned out,
wonderful, shinyful things...

...can be expensive.

VERY expensive indeed.

There just wasn't enough in his saving-up jar...

Oh dear. Poor monster.

What WAS he to do?
It was almost Present Day and there was only one thing worse than a not-perfect present...

and that was
NO PRESENT AT ALL!

Love Monster worried all the way home.

He had NOTHING!

NOTHING to show his perfect monster how much he cared.

But that was when it hit him...
STUFF TO DO INSIDE
BAKING
PERFECT THINGS
PERFECT Things to MAKE & DO for that special someone
BOINK

...perhaps he had EVERYTHING he needed!

He had paints and glitter.

He had some wood and some glue.

And, most important of all, he had AN IDEA!

There was
A LOT
to do.

And
not a lot
of time
to do it.

He worked all night,

until the sun came up.

And when Present Day arrived...

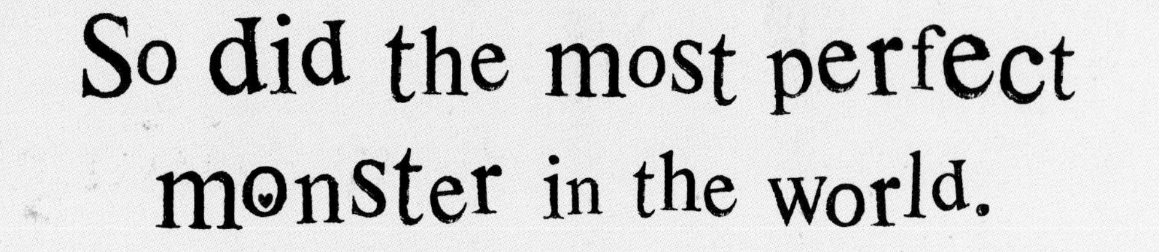

So did the most perfect monster in the world.

And, phew!
Love Monster DID
have something to give.

Something to be very proud of...

You see, sometimes the perfect present doesn't have to cost the earth...

...to mean **the world.**

For my parents, for the gift of life & unconditional love,
my monster, for the gift of us
& Anna & Ali, for friendship & Good times.

Also with special thankyous to my sister for your help & to
Mandy & Helen, for the gift of belief.

First published in paperback in Great Britain by
HarperCollins Children's Books in 2013

1 3 5 7 9 10 8 6 4 2

ISBN: 978-0-00-748791-2

HarperCollins Children's Books is a division of HarperCollins Publishers Ltd.

A CIP catalogue record for this title is available from the British Library.

Visit our website at: www.harpercollins.co.uk

Printed and bound in China